and the
BAFFLED BURGLAR

Reading Consultant: Prue Goodwin, Lecturer in literacy and children's books

ORCHARD BOOKS
338 Euston Road, London NW1 3BH
Orchard Books Australia
Level 17/207 Kent Street, Sydney, NSW 2000

First published in 2012
First paperback publication in 2013

ISBN 978 1 40831 334 3 (hardback)
ISBN 978 1 40831 342 8 (paperback)

A CIP catalogue record for this book is available from the British Library.

1 3 5 7 9 10 8 6 4 2 (hardback)
1 3 5 7 9 10 8 6 4 2 (paperback)

Printed in China

Orchard Books is a division of Hachette Children's Books,
an Hachette UK company.
www.hachette.co.uk

and the
BAFFLED BURGLAR

Justine Smith • Clare Elsom

ORCHARD

Zak Zoo lives at Number One, Africa Avenue. His mum and dad are away on safari, so his animal family is looking after him. Sometimes things get a little . . .

. . . WILL!

Pam

Dad

Mum

Pong

Cressida

Zak

Nanny
Hilda

Lily

Bob

Charlie

Mia (Zak's best friend)

Boris

It was midnight. All around the
house the animals were fast
asleep. Suddenly something made
Zak Zoo wake up.

Zak looked out of the window, but it was very dark. He didn't see the burglar in the garden.

Zak went back to his dream.

Outside, the burglar crept up the
path towards Zak's house.

"One more job," he said, with
a big yawn.

The burglar was tired because he
was always up all night. He never
got enough sleep.

As the burglar crept closer to the house his tummy grumbled. His tummy grumbled because his meal times were back-to-front and upside-down.

He always had his breakfast at
supper time and his supper at
breakfast time, which gave him
bad indigestion.

When the tired burglar got to the house he realised he had left his bag in the car.

"Betty? Betty? Come in, Betty,"
said the burglar. "Betty, bring me
my burglar-bag. Over."

Betty, the burglar's wife, was waiting in the getaway car. She was fast asleep so she didn't hear the burglar calling.

"Never mind," said the burglar.
"I have the burglar-belt that Betty
gave me for my birthday."

The burglar pulled on his gloves.
He wasn't very interested in
burgling – he just liked wearing
the burglar gear.

The burglar loved his burglar gadgets too. Now he checked his new burglar-watch.

When the burglar was inside the house, he called up his wife on the walkie-talkie. "Betty, I'm in!" said the burglar.

He put on his burglar night-goggles
and looked in the mirror. "How do
I look?" he said. Then he saw Pong,
standing right next to him.

He ran into the kitchen and
slammed the door.

"Come IN, Betty," said the burglar.

"Betty, we have a problem! Over!"

Something tapped him lightly on
the shoulder.

"Who . . . who's there?" said the
burglar. What he saw made
him jump.

The burglar dived under the table. "My name isn't Betty, it's Brian!" he said, wiping his brow. Then he looked up and saw Lily.

"Aaargh!" said Brian the burglar, trying to get up. He banged his head on the table.

Upstairs, Zak heard bumping and
shouting and half-woke up.
"I must have been dreaming!"
he said.
He decided to visit the bathroom
before going back to sleep.

Meanwhile, Brian was sneaking up
the stairs.

"What's that noise?" he said.

It was Zak in the bathroom.

"Help!" said Brian, diving into a
cupboard just before Zak came out.

Brian waited until he heard Zak
start to snore.

"Phew!" he said. "I must be safe
now." Then he saw something.
Two sleepy eyes blinked at him
in the dark.

"Wait a minute," he said, feeling for his burglar-belt. He switched on his torch.

"I don't BELIEVE IT!" said Brian, with a sob.

He leapt out of the cupboard.

The burglar flew into the

bathroom . . .

. . . and out again.

He ran down the stairs . . . and
out of the front door.

The burglar rushed out of the
garden and jumped into his car.
Betty drove away at top speed.

In the morning Zak came downstairs and found the night-goggles on the kitchen floor. "Mum must have forgotten to take these on safari with her!" he said.

29

Meanwhile, the burglar decided to stop being a burglar, as he really wasn't very good at it. He and Betty opened a dress-up shop instead, and they were much, much happier.

Zak posted the goggles to his parents, and a few weeks later, he got a letter in reply.

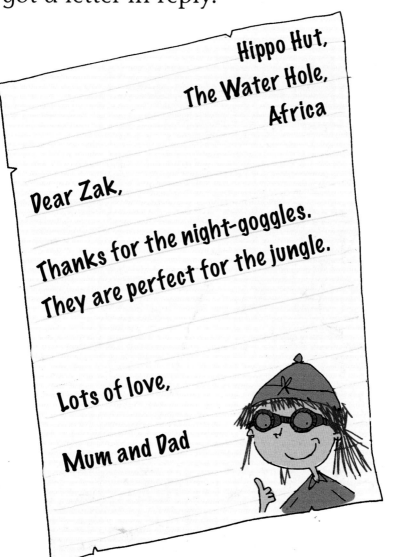

Hippo Hut,
The Water Hole,
Africa

Dear Zak,

Thanks for the night-goggles.
They are perfect for the jungle.

Lots of love,

Mum and Dad

Written by Justine Smith • Illustrated by Clare Elsom

Zak Zoo and the School Hullabaloo	978 1 40831 329 9
Zak Zoo and the Peculiar Parcel	978 1 40831 330 5
Zak Zoo and the Seaside SOS	978 1 40831 331 2
Zak Zoo and the Unusual Yak	978 1 40831 332 9
Zak Zoo and the Hectic House	978 1 40831 333 6
Zak Zoo and the Baffled Burglar	978 1 40831 334 3
Zak Zoo and the TV Crew	978 1 40831 335 0
Zak Zoo and the Birthday Bang	978 1 40831 336 7

All priced at £8.99

Orchard Books are available from all good bookshops,
or can be ordered from our website: www.orchardbooks.co.uk,
or telephone 01235 827702, or fax 01235 827703.

Prices and availability are subject to change.